my itty-bitty bio

Jason Benetti

easterseals

Published in the United States of America by Cherry Lake Publishing Group
Ann Arbor, Michigan
www.cherrylakepublishing.com

Reading Adviser: Beth Walker Gambro, MS, Ed., Reading Consultant, Yorkville, IL
Book Designer: Jennifer Wahi
Illustrator: Jeff Bane

Photo Credits: © University of College/Shutterstock, 5; © BAZA Production/Shutterstock, 7; © Svitlana Ponurkina/ Dreamstime.com, 9; © Carolyn DeVar/Shutterstock, 11; © Jason Benetti, 13, 21; © Dennis Nett/The Post-Standard, 15; © Ron Vesely, 17, 21, 23; Cerebral Palsy Foundation/Youtube AccessibiliTV/Flickr, 19

Library of Congress Cataloging-in-Publication Data

Names: Finke, Beth, 1958- author. | Bane, Jeff, 1957- illustrator.
Title: Jason Benetti / written by Beth Finke ; illustrator Jeff Bane .
Description: Ann Arbor, Michigan : Cherry Lake Publishing, [2023] | Series: My itty-bitty bio | Audience: Grades K-1 | Summary: "Say hello to sportscaster Jason Benetti, the voice of the Chicago White Sox, in this biography for early readers. This book examines his life and impact in a simple, age-appropriate way that helps young readers develop word recognition and reading skills. Developed in partnership with Easterseals and written by a member of the disability community, this title helps all readers learn from those who make a difference in our world. The My Itty-Bitty Bio series celebrates diversity, inclusion, and the values that readers of all ages can aspire to"-- Provided by publisher.
Identifiers: LCCN 2023009100 | ISBN 9781668927298 (hardcover) | ISBN 9781668929810 (ebook) | ISBN 9781668931295 (pdf)
Subjects: LCSH: Benetti, Jason, 1983---Juvenile literature. | Sportscasters--United States--Biography--Juvenile literature. | Cerebral palsied--United States--Biography--Juvenile literature.
Classification: LCC GV742.42.B44 F56 2023 | DDC 796.092 [B]--dc23/eng/20230313
LC record available at https://lccn.loc.gov/2023009100

Printed in the United States of America

table of contents

My Story 4

Timeline 22

Glossary 24

Index 24

The author would like to extend special thanks to Jason Benetti and his agents for their time and participation in the development of this book.

About the author: Beth Finke loves to read and write books. She writes about losing her sight and becoming blind. She also writes about seeing-eye dogs. Her seeing-eye dog, Luna, goes with her to school presentations. Together, they show students the ways guide dogs keep their partners safe from harm. Beth lives in Chicago. She listens to Jason Benetti announce games.

About the illustrator: Jeff Bane and his two business partners own a studio along the American River in Folsom, California, home of the 1849 Gold Rush. When Jeff's not sketching or illustrating for clients, he's either swimming or kayaking in the river to relax.

About our partnership: This title was developed in partnership with Easterseals to support its mission of empowering people with disabilities. Through their national network of affiliates, Easterseals provides essential services and on-the-ground supports to more than 1.5 million people each year.

I was born in Chicago. I nearly died. Doctors saved me. I have **cerebral palsy**.

I walk differently. One of my eyes drifts. That means it moves.

Growing up, I loved sports. But I couldn't play them. My body moves **herky-jerky**.

What are you a fan of?

I watched baseball. I described the game. My voice was strong.

I wrote an essay in school. It was a plan. It said I wanted to be the **TV announcer** for the Chicago White Sox.

Jason

I wonder what my life will
be like twenty years from
now. Mabye I will be
a sportscaster. I would
like to be the White
Sox sportscaster.
As long as I don't look
like Harry Carrey.
I idolize Ken Harrelson
and Tom Paccourk.
I like the idea of
being a sportscaster
when I grow up.
I love the whole
world of sports-
casting. I wonder
how they do it, .. I bet
mabye I will ; you
find out one day will!

People saw how I moved. They didn't think I was smart. So I worked hard.

What do you work hard at?

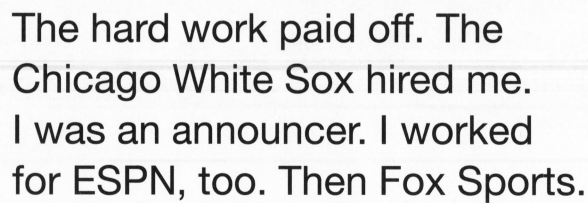

The hard work paid off. The
Chicago White Sox hired me.
I was an announcer. I worked
for ESPN, too. Then Fox Sports.

Some people stare. Some treat me like a kid. I created videos. I made jokes. I want people to understand.

Today, I still love sports. I like doing what people think I can't.

What would you like to ask me?

Jason

I wonder what my life w
be like twenty years fro
now. Mabye I will be
a sportscaster. I would
like to be the White
Sox sportscaster.
As long as I don't s
like Harry Caray.
I idolize Ken Harrelson
and Tom Paciorek.
I like the idea of

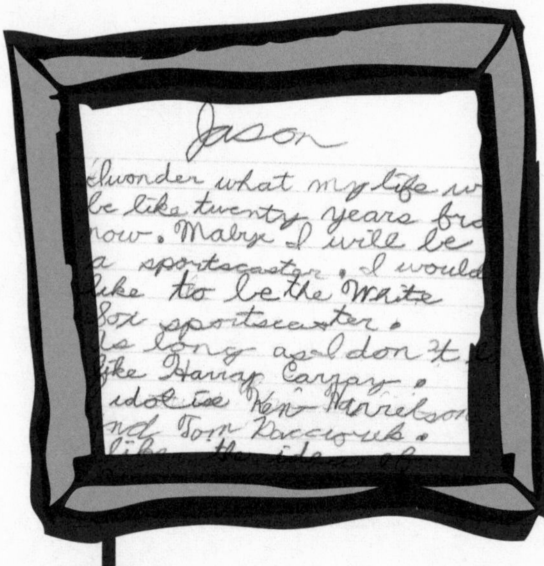

1993

1980

↑
**Born
1983**

2016

2080

glossary

cerebral palsy (suh-REE-brull PAUL-zee) a condition some children are born with that can make it hard for them to stand up straight or move around the way other people do

herky-jerky (HER-key-JUR-key) uneven, unpredictable, not smooth or graceful

TV announcer (tee-vee uh-NOWN-sur) a person who makes announcements describing what you're seeing on the TV screen

index

baseball, 10–13, 16–17

birth, 4, 22

body movement, 6, 8–9, 14

cerebral palsy, 4, 6

Chicago, Illinois, 4–5, 11–13, 17, 21

Chicago White Sox, 10–13, 16–17, 21

disabilities, 4, 6, 8, 18–19

sports, 8, 10–13, 16–17, 20, 21

sportscasters, 10, 12–13, 15–17, 21

timeline, 22–23

videos, 18–19

work ethic, 14–16, 20